Raising a Little Stink

For Sascha Jacob-Alexei – C.S.

To Silvi, whose boundless energy and optimism would give Stinkbug a run for his money – P.C.

Kids Can Press acknowledges the financial support of the Government of Ontario, through the Ontario Media Development Corporation's Ontario Book Initiative; the Ontario Arts Council; the Canada Council for the Arts; and the Government of Canada, through the BPIDP, for our publishing activity.

Published in Canada by
Kids Can Press Ltd.
29 Birch Avenue
Toronto, ON M4V 1E2

Published in the U.S. by
Kids Can Press Ltd.
2250 Military Road
Tonawanda, NY 14150

www.kidscanpress.com

The artwork in this book was rendered in pastel.
The text is set in ClearfaceITC-Regular.

Edited by Jennifer Stokes and Tara Walker
Designed by Céleste Gagnon
Printed and bound in China

This book is smyth sewn casebound.

CM 06 0 9 8 7 6 5 4 3 2 1

Library and Archives Canada Cataloguing in Publication

Sydor, Colleen
Raising a little stink / written by Colleen Sydor ; illustrated by Pascale Constantin.

ISBN-13: 978-1-55337-896-9
ISBN-10: 1-55337-896-2

I. Constantin, Pascale II. Title.

PS8587.Y36R33 2006 jC813'.54 C2005-903653-2

Kids Can Press is a Corus™ Entertainment company

Raising a Little Stink

Colleen Sydor · Pascale Constantin

Kids Can Press

Once there was a lazy old lion who had grown tired of performing at the circus. “Working for a living stinks,” he said to himself, and early the next morning he escaped from his cage and took off into the forest.

Being lazy by nature, the lion soon stopped running and sat down to rest. He rubbed his eyes mightily and yawned widely and, as he did so, a lazy old lion tamer climbed out of his mouth.

The lazy old lion tamer took off his hat to the lion. Then he bowed mightily and stretched widely and, as he did so, a lazy old circus mouse wriggled out of his left breast pocket.

The lazy old circus
mouse grinned widely and
scratched his ear mightily – and
out popped a teeny tiny stinkbug.
The four creatures, happy to be
free at last, set off together in search
of a place to live. Before long they
came upon a small deserted cottage.

"This will have to do," muttered the lion, who was sick and tired of walking.

"A bit small, isn't it?" grumbled the lion tamer, collapsing into a hammock on the porch.

The lazy old circus mouse flopped facedown on a toadstool. "Surely we can do better," he whined.

The teeny tiny stinkbug clasped his hands together and stood on his teeny tiny tippy-toes. "It's positively perfect!" he exclaimed.

The lion, the lion tamer and the circus mouse took to bed immediately. The stinkbug put on an apron and got down to business. He sewed lace curtains for the windows, stenciled wildflowers on the walls and chiseled a wooden plaque that read "Home Sweet Home." Then he repaired a leaky faucet in the kitchen, popped a soufflé in the oven and opened a cookbook in search of a recipe for bananas flambé. After setting the bananas ablaze and putting them aside to cool, he washed his hands and got out his feather duster.

“A stinkbug’s work is never done, is it, Mother?” he said happily, shining her photo with his duster and setting it on the mantle with a sigh.

At first the stinkbug's hard work irritated the others. Just *watching* his efforts made them tired. So they took to watching the television instead. (Without a remote control, however, the lazy creatures were forced to watch the local weather station all day. Not *one* of them would get out of bed to change the channel!)

Eventually the lazy trio's eyes wandered back to the stinkbug, and it didn't take them long to realize that they could put his boundless energies to their own good use.

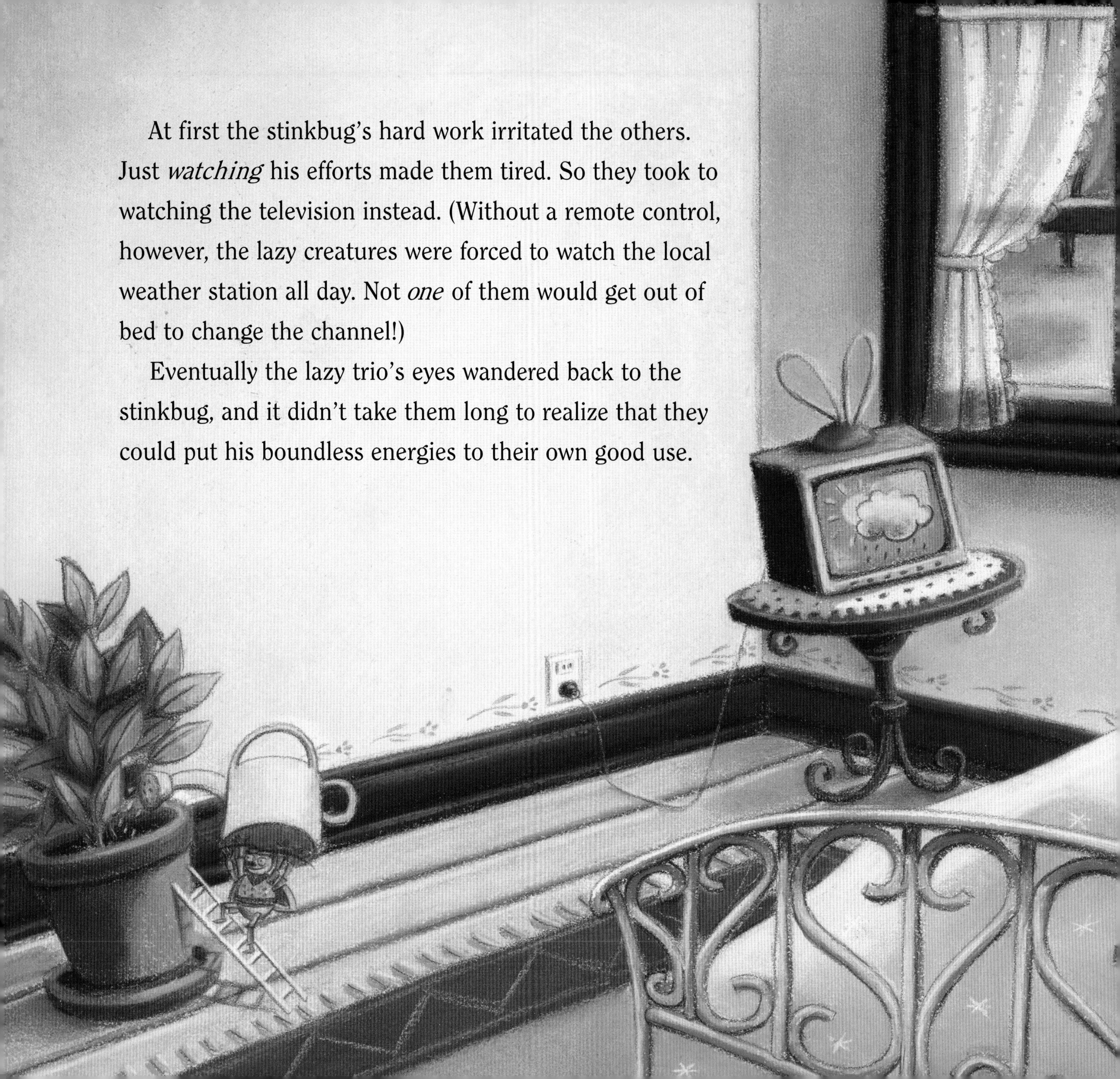

"Stinkbug," called the lion. The stinkbug, who had been busy planting geraniums in the window boxes, stopped his work immediately and went to the lazy old lion's side. "Stinkbug," the lion said, "I have a tremendous craving for some Finger Licky Hot 'n' Sticky Sweet-and-Sour Meatballs. Be a pal and run to the store."

"Sure thing!" said the stinkbug, who had more energy in his teeny tiny pinky than the lion had in his entire body.

He put on his sneakers and jogged fifteen miles to the store for some Finger Licky Hot 'n' Sticky Sweet-and-Sour Meatballs. When he returned, he put the meatballs on a tray and served them to his friends in bed. Then he sat down in the big easy chair to rest.

Soon after, the lazy old lion tamer piped up. "Stinkbug," he called, "these meatballs have given me a terrific thirst. Be a chum and run to the store for some Wild Berry Chokecherry Watermelon Punch."

"Well ... I suppose I could," said the stinkbug. He put his sneakers back on and made the fifteen-mile trek to the store. Looking slightly less than perky upon his return, he nonetheless put a straw and a fancy paper umbrella into each of the three bottles of Wild Berry Chokecherry Watermelon Punch and gave them to the three lazy loafers in bed.

Then he sat down once more in the big easy chair to rest. Just as he was dropping off to sleep, the mouse called to him.

"Stinkbug! I want you to go to the store for me."

The stinkbug put his hands on his hips and narrowed his eyes.

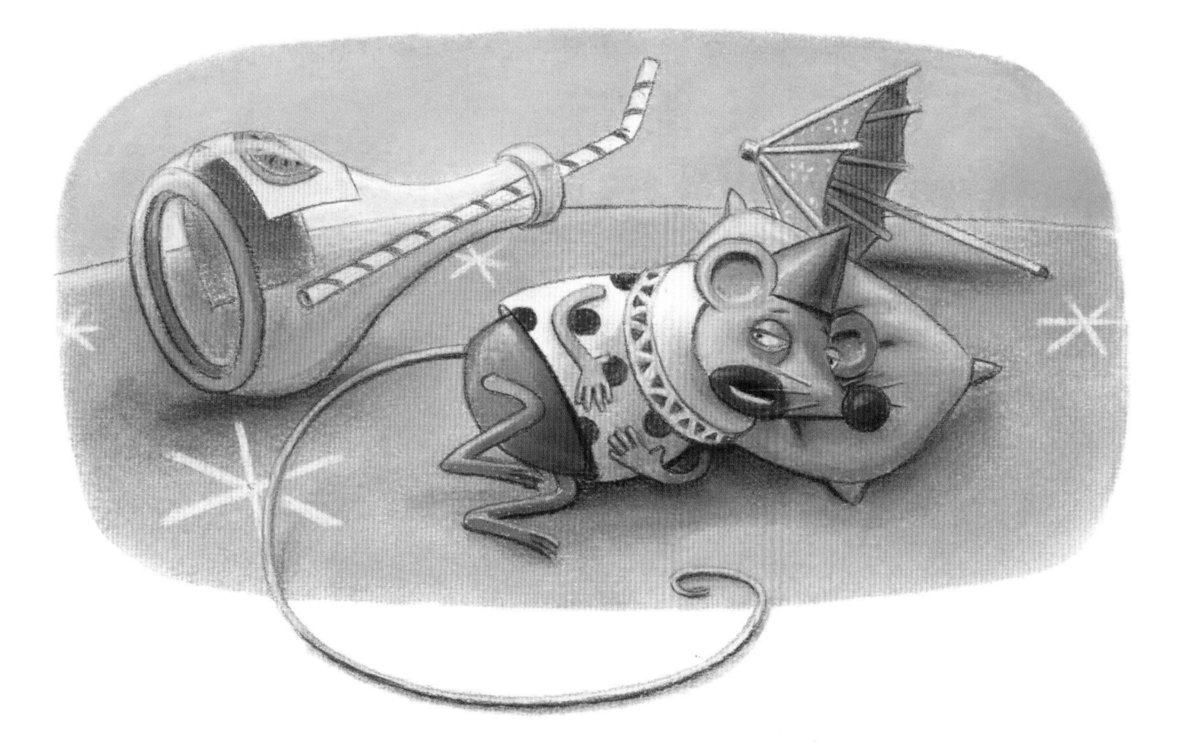

"Please," whimpered the mouse. "It's just that the Finger Licky Hot 'n' Sticky Sweet-and-Sour Meatballs and Wild Berry Chokecherry Watermelon Punch have given me a ferocious tummy ache. I need some chamomile tea."

The stinkbug thought about the many cups of chamomile tea his dear mother had brewed for his own tummy aches over the years.

"Very well," he said with a sigh.

"And while you're in town," added the mouse craftily, "pop into Ernie's Electronics and pick up a remote control for the television!"

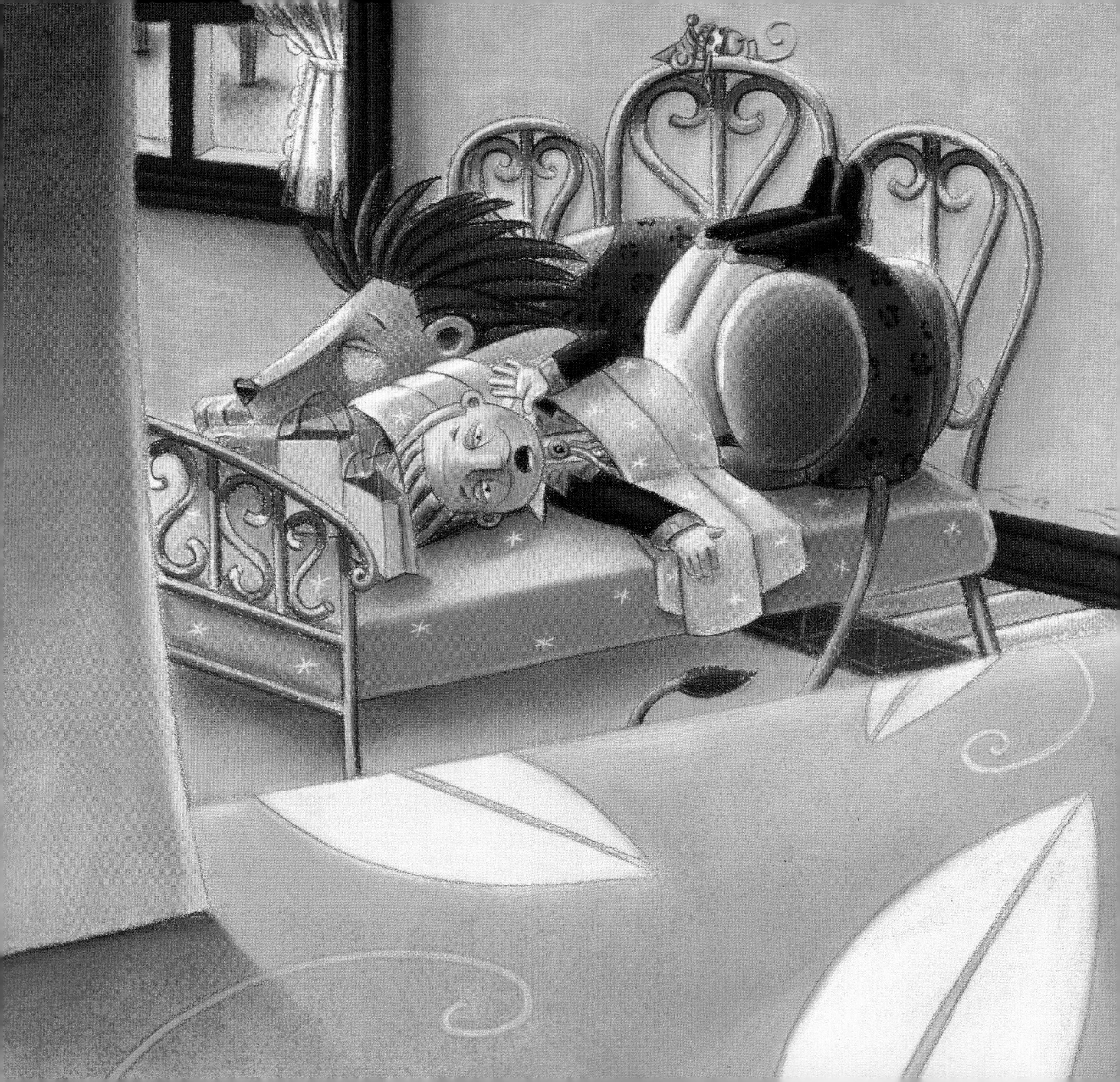

By the time the stinkbug returned, he was perspiring heavily. He threw the shopping bags on the bed and flumped into the big easy chair.

"Stinkbug!" called the lion tamer.

But the stinkbug did not respond, for although he was extremely good-natured, he was definitely nobody's fool. The stinkbug had no intention of leaving his easy chair.

"Stinkbug!" called the mouse.

No response.

"Stinkbug!" roared the lion. "Are you *deaf?*"

Not a peep.

Reluctantly, the three lazy creatures dragged themselves from their bed and gathered around the stinkbug's chair.

"STINKBUG!"

they screeched.

This time he *did* respond. His friends watched, fascinated, as the stinkbug squeezed his eyes shut and began thrumming his wings so furiously that they were sure he was about to lift off.

Instead, slowly, *very* slowly, the room began to fill with a tremendous stink.

The lion, the lion tamer and the mouse looked at each other with wide eyes and drooping jaws. Never, *ever*, in all their days had they encountered such a strong and disagreeable odor. They fanned the air widely and plugged their noses mightily, but it was no use.

To escape the wretched smell, the mouse jumped into the lion tamer's pocket, the lion tamer jumped into the lion's mouth and the lion ran all the way back to the circus and jumped into his empty cage.

And that is where the three lazy creatures remain to this very day, for, as the lion likes to point out, working for a living may stink, but it's a bed of *roses* compared to living with a little stinker.

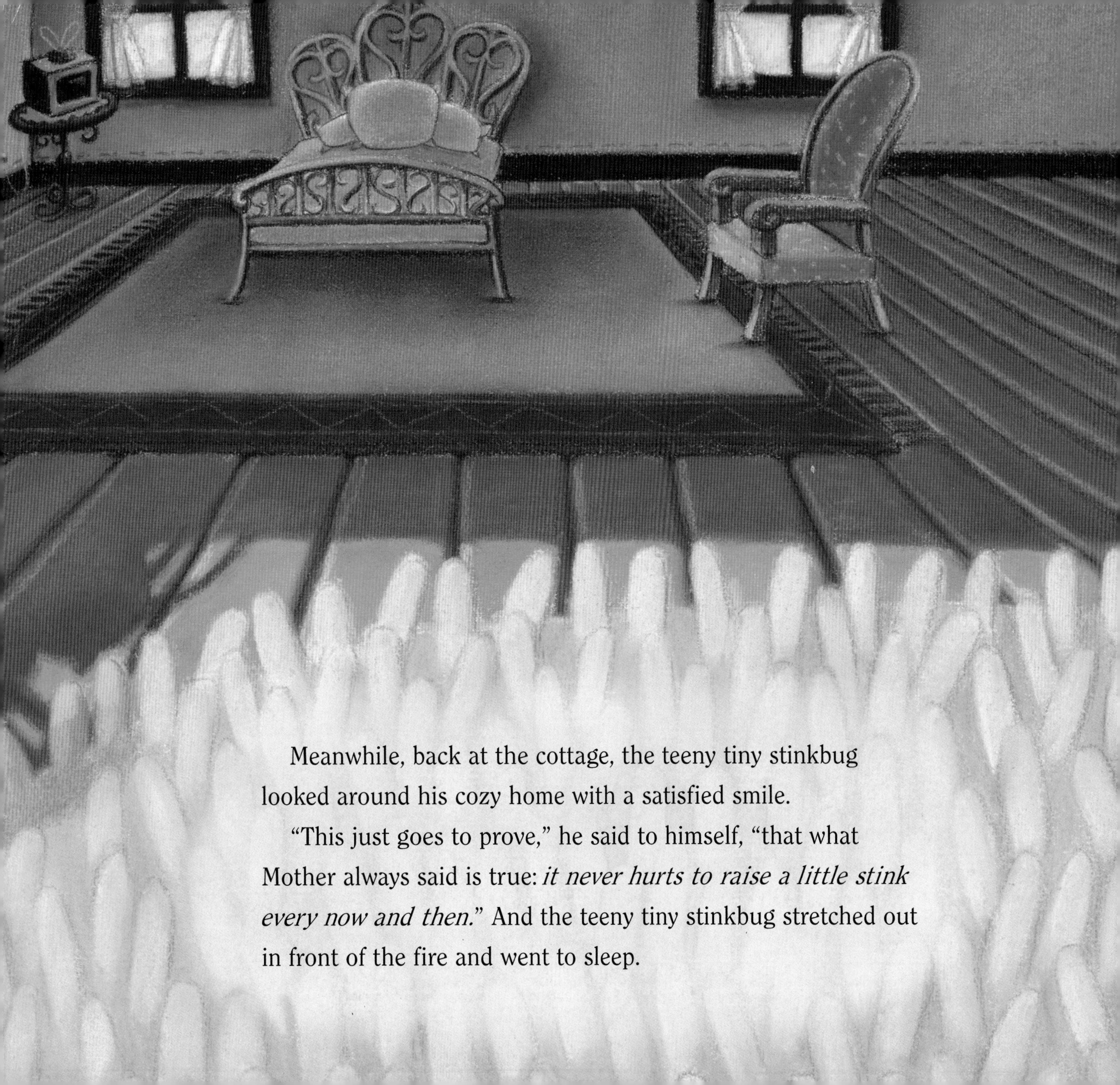

Meanwhile, back at the cottage, the teeny tiny stinkbug looked around his cozy home with a satisfied smile.

"This just goes to prove," he said to himself, "that what Mother always said is true: *it never hurts to raise a little stink every now and then.*" And the teeny tiny stinkbug stretched out in front of the fire and went to sleep.

Working Stinks!
Stinking Works!